TERRY
DEARY'S
TERRIBLY TRUE
SPY STORIES

SCHOLASTIC

The facts behind these stories are true. However, they have been dramatized to make them into gripping stories, and some of the characters are fictitious.

Thanks to the Portgordon Cultural Heritage Group for the original story of "The Apple Spy".

Scholastic Children's Books,
Euston House, 24 Eversholt Street
London, NW1 1DB

A division of Scholastic Ltd
London ~ New York ~ Toronto ~ Sydney ~ Auckland
Mexico City ~ New Delhi ~ Hong Kong

First published in the UK under the series title *True Stories*
by Scholastic Ltd, 1998
This edition published 2006

All rights reserved

Typeset by Rapid Reprographics Ltd
Printed by Nørhaven Paperback A/S, Denmark

10 9 8 7 6 5 4 3

CONTENTS

INTRODUCTION

My name is Bond, James Bond, but you can call me 007. Well, that's not true. My name is not James Bond, and James Bond never existed. But we can all dream and spying seems a dream job … *if* you believe all you see in the cinema and read in the books.

Spies seem so glamorous. Their lives are full of excitement and they are always such heroes! They are working for their country against an evil enemy who is out to destroy them. They are snatching secrets from under the noses of some foreign secret police and bringing them home. They are our guardian angels.

Of course enemy spies are not so glamorous, are they? They are traitors who sneak about, lying, murdering and stealing from our country. Enemy spies will use any low and dirty trick you can imagine to get their hands on our secrets. They are the worst devils of our nightmares.

Spies are angels – when they are on our side. Spies are devils when they work for the enemy. What is the truth? Would you like to be a spy? There is only one way to find out. Forget about James Bond for a while. Look at some true spy stories. Study the people who have lived and died as spies, the way they worked, the sort of things they had to do.

Spies have been around for thousands of years. Did you know that there are spy stories in the Bible? In one story, a Persian called Zopyrus wanted to get inside Babylon and let his Persian army in. He walked up to the gates of Babylon and said, "I want to join you. I hate the Persians. I tried to talk them out of attacking Babylon so they cut off my ears and my nose and whipped me till I bled."

The Babylonians believed Zopyrus and let him into the city – as soon as he had the chance the sneaky Zopyrus opened the gates of Babylon and let in his Persian friends.

How could the Babylonians have been so stupid as to believe this lying spy? Because they saw he had no nose, no ears and his back was raw with whipping. If *you* saw this horrid sight then wouldn't you believe he hated the Persians for doing that to him?

The *truth* about Zopyrus the spy is too amazing to believe. Zopyrus whipped himself, cut off his own nose and lopped off his own ears just to get into Babylon.

What a hero – to the Persians.

Could *you* do that for *your* country? Can you imagine James Bond cutting off his nose? No! Because James Bond stories are make-believe and Zopyrus's is a true spy story. If you want to know more true spy stories then read them here.

ALEXANDER THE GREATEST

Spying is about gathering information and stealing secrets. Leaders want to know what their enemies are up to. In the 1500s, Queen Elizabeth had one of the world's first spy organizations run by her spy-master Sir Francis Walsingham. But before that, rulers had to come up with their own plots. Alexander the Great was a master of secret schemes. Some say he murdered his own father to get control of the kingdom. He then went on to conquer Greece and Persia. He was the master of the greatest empire in the world, but he still wasn't safe. Alexander had no spy-master like Sir Francis Walsingham. He had to do it all for himself...

Date: 327 BC
Place: Persia

The man was barefoot and dirty. His hair was matted and his body was covered in sores. His body was hunched and he looked over his shoulder every few steps. At last he arrived at the magnificent silk tent. "I've come to see the emperor," he croaked.

The guard looked at him with disgust but lowered his spear and nodded for the man to enter the tent. Alexander was lying on a couch and studying a map when the shabby man slid in. He looked up sharply. The emperor was a young man, but the strain of the fighting and the constant danger had given him hard lines at the edge of his large eyes and firm mouth. "Did anyone see you?"

"No, sir," the man said in a soft whine.

Alexander rested his hand on the hilt of the dagger at his belt. "It had better be important," he said menacingly.

"It is, sir."

"Quickly then, what is it?"

"It's some of your men, sir. They're not happy."

The emperor swung his feet to the floor and planted a strong hand on the map. "I have given them Greece and its wealth," he said, jabbing at the map with his finger. He moved it to the right. "We've conquered Persia and its riches. Now we're going to take India and enough of its treasures to make them rich for life," he said, sweeping his fingers to the south-east. "What more do they want?"

"They want to go home, sir."

Alexander's lip curled in a sneer. "Over my dead body."

The man in the tattered tunic clasped his hands tightly. "I think that's what they are planning, sir," he whispered.

His master snorted. "So, it's come to that, has it? They plan to murder me and run home to their dear little wives and mothers, do they?"

"That's what I heard them plan, sir."

"Which men are leading the plot?"

"Oh, I can't tell you that, sir. They wouldn't let a camp-follower like me into their great tents, sir. I only know what I heard through the tent walls."

"Didn't you recognize the voices?"

The man shook his head sadly. "No, sir."

"Get out," Alexander ordered. As the man backed slowly towards the door the emperor reached into a leather pouch and took out a coin. He threw it on to the floor. The man snatched it with a stained hand and ran out into the night. Alexander lay back on his couch, closed his eyes and rested a hand on his brow. The only sound was the sputtering of oil lamps and the distant barking of dogs on guard at the edge of the camp.

After a long while he rose slowly and walked to the opening of the tent. "Fetch General Parmenion," he snapped. The guard woke from his doze and pulled himself to attention.

Parmenion had been asleep when his leader's message came. He threw on a tunic and sandals and limped through the rows of tents by the light of the dying camp-fires. He combed his grey hair with his fingers and entered Alexander's tent. He saluted quickly and waited.

"Parmenion," Alexander said warmly. "Sit down, my friend."

The general sat on the couch, while Alexander paced the floor of the tent. "Sorry to wake you."

"I'm used to it," the old soldier laughed. "You've had one of your ideas, I suppose."

"Yes, Parmenion. I am worried about the men being so far from home. We've been away from Greece for two years now. Some of the men must be getting a little homesick."

"They worry about their families, of course," Parmenion said. "Don't we all?"

"I have my son Nicias alongside me," the general smiled. "I'm one of the lucky ones."

"You *are*. But I thought it might be good for the men to get in touch with their families. I thought I'd arrange to have a wagon sent home to deliver their letters."

Parmenion shrugged. "We've tried it before, but the wagons have always been attacked and robbed by bandits on land or pirates at sea. Writing those letters was just a waste of time."

"But this time it would be different. This time I would send it with a strong armed guard."

Parmenion gave a broad smile. "That is marvellous, sir. It will be very popular with the men."

12

Alexander looked up sharply. "Am I not popular now?"

Parmenion's smile faded. "Oh! Of course, Emperor! The men love you!"

"*All* of the men?"

"*All* of them," Parmenion cried.

Alexander slapped a hand on his general's shoulder. "You are a good man, Parmenion. Too good at times. You see only the good in our friends. You don't see the bad. But I trust you, Parmenion. Of all the officers in this army, you're the only one I trust."

"Thank you, sir."

"I'll announce the mail wagon tomorrow at the planning meeting. It will leave tomorrow evening."

The next morning, Alexander explained his plan to send letters back to Greece and told his officers that the day would be a rest day. They could spend the time writing. "I promise you, the letters will be safe in my care. I have selected the men who will escort the wagon. There are no better men in this army."

As evening fell on the dusty plain, the mail wagon was loaded and was placed in the middle of a convoy of heavily armed soldiers with their own baggage and supplies wagons. The order was given to leave and the company set off slowly towards the setting sun.

After half an hour, the camp was out of sight and the road took the wagons into some low hills. A man sat on top of one hill and watched them pass below him, then he rode slowly down towards the lumbering horses. The driver stopped and saluted. "Good evening, Emperor."

"Good evening, Captain," Alexander said, and he smiled grimly. "Stop here for a while. Give the men food but no wine – I want them awake for the rest of the night. And light some torches so I can read."

The company dismounted and began to gather wood for fires, while their emperor pulled the parcels of letters from the wagon and began to open them. After an hour Alexander had two piles of letters. He picked up the smaller pile and called the commander of the company across to him. "These letters here are the ones that have the information I want. The writers have told their loved ones all about a plot to kill me and return home. Some have very kindly listed all the men who are part of the plot. Of course they will have to die."

"Yes, sir."

"I've made a list of the names. I want you to leave the wagons here and return to the camp on horseback with me. We'll take these men while they are asleep. There will be no need for any trials. You will bring them to me one at a time, I will listen to their confessions in my tent, and then you will take them outside and execute them. Do you understand?"

"Perfectly, Emperor."

"Then let's make ready."

It was deep into the night when the sleepy and confused plotters were dragged from their beds and held under close guard until Alexander was ready to see them. Parmenion hurried from the comfort of his bed for the second night running and dashed into Alexander's tent. "What is happening, Emperor?"

Alexander held up one of the letters. "We have traitors in our midst, Parmenion."

The general read the letter quickly and his face creased with pain. "Hippothales? A traitor? Who'd have thought it?" he cried.

"I told you that you trusted people too much, Parmenion. But it is there in his own writing. I have to execute him and the other men on my list."

"Of course you do," the general said. "They deserve it."

"I'm glad you agree," Alexander said softly. Then he called, "Bring in the first traitor!"

The guards led a young officer into the tent. His face was bruised and bleeding from the struggle he'd put up when he was arrested. Parmenion looked at the young man and turned pale. "Nicias!" he moaned.

"Yes," Alexander nodded. "Your son." The emperor looked at the prisoner. "Have you anything to say, Nicias?"

The young man raised his chin so he looked down on the emperor. "You are a tyrant and an evil man, Alexander. You are not satisfied with conquering half of the world. You want it all!"

Alexander nodded slowly. "I conquered half the world by being ruthless with anyone who stood in my way. And that's how I'll conquer the other half. You'll have to die so I can live."

"I'm not afraid."

Alexander laughed suddenly. "Hah! And *I'm* not afraid to die *some* day. I'm just not ready to die yet. It's such a waste."

"Then let him live," Parmenion put in quickly.

The emperor frowned. "Moments ago you agreed that these traitors should all die."

Parmenion hung his head. When he raised it again his eyes were filled with tears. His son was being hauled out of the tent and he took a step to follow. Two of Alexander's bodyguards seized his arms and held him back. Alexander walked across to

15

him and stood very close. "If I have the son killed, then the father will have a duty to avenge his son ... won't you, Parmenion?"

"Yes."

"So, even though you didn't plot against me, I will have to have you killed too. You understand, don't you?"

"Yes."

The emperor's large, dark eyes softened. "Nicias was wrong, my friend. It's not *enough* to be ruthless and cruel. If you want to rule the world you need something else. You need cunning. You must trust no one, Parmenion. Especially not the ones who say they are your friends. Watch their every move and set traps. Spy out their secrets and know everything. That's the way to rule the world, Parmenion." He stretched out his arms and held the old general close for a few moments. "Goodbye, my friend. Goodbye."

Alexander was so upset by the execution of Parmenion and the other plotters that he refused to eat for a week. In the end he was force-fed by his friends.

The emperor wasn't the only famous person to become a spy. There have been many people who were famous for other things but were also spies. People like London Lord Mayor Dick Whittington, who spied for his king on foreign travels and England's first great poet, Geoffrey Chaucer, who wrote spy reports in a secret code. These are just a few of the ones we know about...

Famous Spies

1. **Mithradates the Great, 132–63 BC.** This teenage king of Turkey fled from assassins and disguised himself as a beggar. He had learned 22 languages by the age of 14 – always useful for a spy – and wandered through Turkish cities studying their defences. After a few years he knew all about those defences and the weaknesses of the cities. He returned and, with his small army, easily overran the cities and reclaimed his throne. Mithradates' mother and brother had been ruling the country – he had them executed.

2. **Marcus Licinius Crassus, 115–53 BC.** This Roman ruled the Empire alongside Julius Caesar. He set up schools for slaves, and the educated slaves were given jobs with the most important Romans. They also spied on those top Romans and reported their secrets to Crassus. He used those secrets to make himself rich and to keep himself safe from his enemies. When Crassus led an army against Parthia he didn't bother to use spies and was defeated. His head was cut off and his mouth filled with molten gold.

3. **King Alfred the Great, AD 849–899.** Alfred was the leader of the Saxons in England at a time when the Danes were taking over the country. One story says that Alfred dressed himself as a minstrel and wandered into the Danish camp. He entertained them and stayed for their feast, during which they talked about

F
A
C
T

F
I
L
E

their battle plans. Next day Alfred slipped out of the camp and prepared the Saxon army to defeat the plans he'd overheard. Sadly, this story was first written down 500 years after Alfred's death so there's no way of checking if it's true.

4. **Christopher Marlowe, 1564–93.** This playwright could have been as great as William Shakespeare. The trouble was that he seemed to enjoy spying as much as writing. He worked for Elizabeth I's spy-master, Sir Francis Walsingham, and his job was to uncover Catholic plots against the Queen. Like many other spies, his masters suspected he was working secretly for the enemy – the Catholics. In a meeting with three of Walsingham's spies, Marlowe was stabbed in the eye and died. The spies claimed it was a quarrel – some historians think Marlowe was executed because his spy-masters mistrusted him.

5. **Daniel Defoe, 1660–1731.** This English writer was not popular with the government because he wrote offensive things about them. After a spell in prison he offered to work for the government and train spies. These spies would report on exactly who was making trouble in Britain. Defoe's secret agents were trained to mix with the population and seem quite ordinary – then betray their friends. It was Britain's first real secret service. He was able to give up spying when one of his books became a great success – the famous Robinson Crusoe.

6. **Benjamin Franklin, 1706–90.** A famous scientist who tried to be a double agent. He was one of the founders of the American spy network and pretended to be working for them in the War of Independence. In fact, he was passing on their secrets to the British. Then, when it was clear that the Americans were going to win the war, he rejoined the American side. One of the American leaders, John Quincy Adams, suspected Franklin of betraying his country but he didn't have enough evidence. Franklin survived to become a hero of American science.

7. **Sir Robert Baden-Powell, 1857–1941.** From 1880 until 1902 this army officer used his skill as an actor to enter enemy territory in disguise. In Hercegovina he pretended to be a butterfly collector while collecting plans of enemy gun positions, and in Hamburg he pretended to be a drunk to get details of German warships. He became a spy-trainer, using Zulus to spy on the Dutch during the Boer Wars in South Africa. He wrote a book called Aids to Scouting in 1899 and it was used to train boy-soldiers. This later gave him the idea of creating the Boy Scout organization – and that's what he is remembered for.

8. **Mata Hari, 1876–1917.** This Dutch woman was a very popular dancer in the early 1900s and had many important

FACT FILE

admirers. Mata Hari was able to learn French and British secrets and was accused of selling them to Germany during World War I. Mata Hari offered to work for the French Secret Service but they accused her of betraying them. The French put her on trial and she was sentenced to death by firing squad. Bravely she refused to have a blindfold. The truth is that she never learned any dangerous secrets and never betrayed anyone.

THE CULPER RING

Think of spies and you think of agents living with the enemy, secret messages written in code with invisible ink, and clever ways of arranging for letters to be picked up. Not many true spy stories have these interesting features ... but one story has them all! The place was New York in 1780. The victim was the British Army. The spies were the Americans who wanted independence from British rule. This is the story of one vital message that got through, thanks to a group of American spies who became known as the Culper Ring.

Date: 1780
Place: New York

The woman was small and slim. Her bright eyes sparkled with excitement as she ran up the stairs to the room above the store and threw open the door. "Robert! Robert!" she cried. "I've heard the most amazing thing."

Robert Townsend looked up from the table. His red-brown hair was cut short and pulled back into a ribbon at the back of his head. He raised his cleft chin and looked down his long nose at her. Without speaking, he rose to his feet, crossed to the door and looked down the stairs. Then he closed the door quietly and returned to his seat at the table. His tired eyes had dark shadows under them and made him look older than his 25 years.

"Now, quietly, my dear. What have you heard?"

She sat across the table from him and leaned forward eagerly. "The British are planning to attack our friends the French at Newport! We have to warn the French!"

Robert looked at her calmly. "They will want to strike before the French can join up with our American forces," he nodded. "It would be disastrous for us. Are you sure of this?"

"The British major told me himself. He was boasting about it!"

"Then we must send a message to our general to warn him," Robert said calmly. He walked to a cupboard and took out a small ink bottle, a quill pen and a blank sheet of paper. The woman watched as he dipped the quill in the pot and began to write. She watched, fascinated, as his pen touched the paper and the liquid vanished. "What are you saying?" she demanded.

He spoke as he wrote. "To 321. This 356 is to say that 355 reports our friends in 727 plan an advance on 644. Take 356 to 711 without delay."

She smiled and nodded. "To the spy chief. This letter is to say that 355 – that's me – reports our friends in New York – that's the British – plan an advance on the French. Take letter to our general without delay."

When he had finished the sheet of paper looked as blank as before he had started. "You've done well," he said, but still he didn't smile at the bright-eyed woman. "Stay here. 724 is due here in an hour."

Robert walked slowly down the stairs into the store and took his place behind the counter. When his assistant, Henry Oakman, left to have some dinner, Robert took the sheet of paper from under his jacket and placed it on the counter. He took a packet of paper from a shelf, opened it carefully and counted out 19 sheets. Robert placed his own sheet at number 20 and slipped it back into the packet, then sealed it.

Oakman had returned and was serving some British soldiers when Austin Roe strolled into the shop. He grinned at the soldiers. "Morning, gentlemen!" he said cheerfully and raised his hat to them. Then he turned to Robert Townsend and brought out a slip of paper. He slid it across the counter, under the noses of the British soldiers and said, "My order, Master Townsend."

Robert picked up the paper and tried to control the trembling in his hand. All that appeared on the paper were the words, "Will you please send one ream of letter paper, the same as the last shipment." The storekeeper knew that between the lines of the message was another written in invisible ink. He folded the note carelessly and stuffed it into a pouch at the front of his apron. Then he reached beneath the counter and found the packet of paper he'd prepared earlier. He passed it across to Austin Roe.

"There you are, Master Roe," he said. He couldn't say too much with the British in the shop. "I guess it will be an urgent order, is it? You'll be hurrying back with it, won't you?"

He pulled a face. "I have just ridden fifty miles for this order and now you want me to ride straight back?"

Robert's face was wooden. "That's right. You'll want to be in Setauket before nightfall. There are all sorts of strange folk out on the roads these days."

"Bandits, you mean?" Austin cried. The British soldiers looked at him and he smiled back. "I know I'm safe so long as the British army is in control."

The soldiers nodded seriously. Austin Roe turned away from them so they didn't see the huge wink he gave to Robert Townsend. "Give my regards to your lovely wife," he said happily and walked out of the shop with the packet of paper underneath his arm.

He walked along the waterfront towards the tavern. Robert's shop was in a good position there. He could stand behind his counter and watch all the British ships that arrived and left. That was what usually went in his reports. Austin Roe guessed that today there was something more urgent. He collected a fresh horse from the tavern and had a hasty meal before he rode quickly out of the city on the road to Setauket.

The sentry on the road from New York stopped Austin, as he knew he would. "Where are you going?"

"Good afternoon, Sergeant! A fine day, isn't it?"

The British soldier was not going to be fooled by Austin Roe's cheerful greeting. "I asked you where you were going."

"Back home to Setauket. I've just been collecting supplies from New York. Paper for my master's business. You can examine it if you like."

"Make sure you go straight home," the sour-faced soldier said, and let him through.

Austin's excitement gave him all the energy he needed to climb off his horse four hours later and run up the steps of the front porch to his house. "Good journey?" his wife called.

"Safe enough. But the British are nervous about something. They're checking everyone." He laid the packet of paper on his table, looked up at her worried face and smiled. He patted the parcel. "It's safe enough," he said and began to open it. He pulled out the 20th sheet. It looked as blank as the rest but he sniffed at it and the faint scent of chemicals told him it was the right one. He folded it carefully and placed it inside his jacket. "I'll pass it on and be back for supper in twenty minutes," he said.

"It'll be ready," his wife told him.

Austin walked to the end of his row of houses and opened the gate into a field of cows. He'd been away for a day in New York – no one would be surprised to see him checking his beasts in the field he rented from little Abraham Woodhull.

Austin checked each animal patiently then made his way across to the far corner of the field. There was a hollow there and he was out of sight of prying eyes. He dropped quickly to his knees, brushed earth away with his hand and uncovered the lid of a wooden box. He flipped up the lid, dropped the paper inside, closed it and covered it with soil again. Then he returned home to his hard-earned supper.

No one would be surprised to see Abraham Woodhull cross the field half an hour later. But everyone who knew him would be amazed to know he was American Agent 722, code-named Culper, and head of the Culper spy ring. Abraham was a pale-faced, trembling little man who was scared of his own shadow. He lived in terror of being discovered and that terror often drove him to his sickbed. That evening his whole body shook as he crossed the field, slipped the paper from its hiding- place and hurried back to his room in the lodging house. He passed the door to the room where two British officers lived, and his trembling legs almost failed to carry him on up the stairs to his own room.

It was cool now that the sun had set, but Abraham was sweating as he locked the door and turned up the wick on his oil lamp. He took a bottle of liquid from his desk and carefully brushed it over the blank paper. Slowly Robert Townsend's message appeared. "My God!" he gasped and looked close to fainting. He swayed as he walked across to his window and opened it. The fresh air helped to revive him but it wasn't the air he wanted. It was a clear view of Anna Strong's clothes-line across the bay. There was a black petticoat fluttering there, almost invisible now that darkness was falling. He knew what that meant. "Caleb Brewster the boatman's in town," he mumbled. He strained his watery eyes to count the number of handkerchiefs on the same line. "One ... two ... three ... beached in the third bay."

This was the dangerous part. Now that the invisible message could be read he had to get it to Caleb before anyone else saw it. He pulled a cloak from a wall cupboard and shrugged his feeble body into it. He crept past the British officers' door. He was on tiptoe so they wouldn't hear him pass. He breathed again when he was past it then turned in horror as the door was pulled open. "Abraham!" a young blond-haired officer cried.

"What? What?"

"What are you doing, creeping around in the dark like a thief in the night?"

"I need a walk. Air. Fresh air. Feel faint. Need a walk! Along the cliffs."

"You need some company, Abraham, in case you fall over the edge. From the look of you it could happen!"

"No! Fine. I'm fine I am. Fresh air. I'll be fine."

The British officer slapped his back. "You take care, my friend."

"Yes. Fine. I'll take care. Good care!" and his voice was little more than a squeak.

Abraham knew that it would take him a day or two in bed to recover from this night, but he had to do this for his country. The fresh air really did make him feel a little better, and he strode along the cliffs till he came to the bay where a whale-boat was pulled up on the shore. He could have probably climbed down the rough cliff path but he knew he'd never get back up. He was relieved to see the red glow and drifting sparks from Caleb Brewster's pipe as his messenger sat at the top of the cliff.

"Good evening, Caleb. A fine night for fishing."

"Aye," the broad-shouldered seaman nodded.

"Fine enough to row all the way to Connecticut."

"That's where I'm headed."

All the while Agent 722 Abraham Woodhull was looking back towards Setauket to see if he was being followed. When he was sure he was quite safe, he pulled the letter from his coat and thrust it into Caleb's huge hand. "It is very urgent, Caleb, and very important. You must get it there by morning!"

Even in the weak light from a chip of moon Abraham could see the surprise on Caleb's face. "Have I ever let you down, Abraham?"

Abraham felt a little guilt in himself and a warm pride in his colleague. "Never, Caleb, never."

"Get yourself back in the warm and don't worry, Abraham."

The little man felt a huge weight lifted off his shoulders as the boatman slid down the cliff path and he was able to return to his lodging with an empty pocket. By the next morning the message was with 321 – Colonel Benjamin Tallmadge, the American spy chief in Newport, Connecticut. Within a few hours it was in the hands of the American Army commander, 711. The commander was also the general who had set up the Caleb Circle.

The general's name was George Washington.

Washington's spy, 355, had got her message through to him.

It was a complicated way to send messages, but it had proved safe in the past. This message, the most important that 355 had ever sent, was safe too.

Washington called his officers together. "The British are leaving New York to attack our friends the French. How can we stop them?"

"Attack New York and make the British race back to defend it," one officer suggested.

Washington nodded. "That's what we'll do."

"But we haven't enough men," someone argued.

The general gave a grim smile. "How many do we need?"

"Twelve thousand at least."

George Washington nodded. He picked up a quill and wrote quickly while his officers watched silently. "There you are. An order for 12,000 Americans to attack New York in two days' time." He passed the paper to his senior officer. "I want this message to fall into the hands of the British. I want it handed to a man the British trust. Do we have a spy in the British camp that they trust?"

"Yes, sir," Tallmadge said. "He's a farmer. They are sure he is one of them."

Washington said calmly, "I want them to think this really is an order coming from me."

"Then we aren't going to attack New York?" someone asked.

"There's no need. When the British read this they will give up the attack on the French. We will go and march to meet our allies and have a force strong enough to drive the British out." The man who had created the Culper Ring looked around at his officers. "Gentlemen, we will win this war. But we won't win it because we have the biggest army or the best weapons. We will win it because we know more about the enemy than the enemy knows about us. You soldiers will get the medals, but the real heroes will be the ones who risk their lives to spy for their country. Remember them, gentlemen. Remember them."

Washington's plan worked perfectly. The British believed his fake message and missed the chance to attack the French when they were at their weakest. Washington's Americans went on to win their fight for independence.

The men of the Culper Ring are heroes – but no one has ever discovered the name of their greatest spy. The woman, an American heroine, who will forever be known simply as 355.

The Culper story is a good example of secret ways of sending information. A vital thing for spies...

F

A

C

T

F

I

L

E

Spy Messages

1. Invisible ink has been used for thousands of years and has been made from milk, vinegar, lemon juice and even urine! A World War I Belgian spy wrote an invisible-ink message on the back of a woman and sent her through German defences. Sadly she was caught, the message was uncovered and she was shot.

The problem was that messages in secret inks had to be kept quite short. They are still used but have been largely replaced by radio messages and miniature photographs.

2. In 1853, French inventor Prudent Dagron used a special camera to shrink a picture of a page to a small dot. He had invented a top spy tool – the "microdot". Of course, carrying the messages was a different problem. Dagron rolled a strip of 3,000 microdots into a tube and fastened it to the tail of a homing pigeon. It worked. Today a message can be reduced 40,000 times, so a 300-page book can be printed on a postage stamp.

3. One of the first people to use pigeons was Julius Caesar in 50 BC, to send reports home to Rome. By World War I the birds had miniature cameras

F A C T

F I L E

strapped to them so they could be flown over enemy defences to photograph them. In World War II British pigeons were dropped on miniature parachutes to agents in France. The agents made their reports and the pigeons took them back to Britain. German soldiers soon learned about this and had orders to shoot any suspicious-looking pigeons. The heroic pigeons that did get home safely were often eaten once their message had been read!

4. In World War I a German spy used a dog to carry messages across the British trenches to his friends. It then returned with food and water to the spy's hiding-place. British soldiers saw the dog jumping the trenches every night and at first thought it was a phantom. Then the spy died and the howling dog was discovered. British Intelligence Officers tried to catch it but failed several times ... though they did trap one another in their clumsy nets. At last a soldier came up with the answer – he took a female dog along one night and the lonely spy dog couldn't resist walking into the trap.

5. Morse Code was invented in the 1840s for sending messages by telegraph or by flashing lights. It has been replaced by newer methods of sending messages and is no longer used. But for over 100 years it was a valuable spy tool.

A French woman agent wanted to pass on a message to an English spy in a café in 1914 and didn't want to be overheard. She came up with the idea of blinking at him in Morse Code! A brilliant spy idea! Sadly the Englishman had never learned the code.

6. Opper de Blowitz was a reporter for the British newspaper, *The Times*. In 1878 he got an amazing amount of information to London about a meeting in Berlin that was supposed to be secret. One of the members of the meeting was passing information to de Blowitz. Enemy agents tailed the reporter but never caught him meeting anyone, sending letters or picking up packages from secret locations. How did he do it? Every day he and his informer went to the same restaurant for lunch – they never sat together or spoke. But they each hung up their top hat as they went into the restaurant, and picked up the other one's hat as they left. The enemy agents never spotted the switch.

F
A
C
T

F
I
L
E

7. A Greek called Histiaeus was imprisoned by the Persians but was allowed to send a slave with a letter to his cousin Aristagoras. The Persians read the letter but could see no code or secret meaning. The message was a perfectly harmless letter. They let the slave take the letter to Aristagoras. As soon as the slave arrived he said to Aristagoras, "Shave my head." The real message was tattooed on his scalp. This idea was still being used during World War II.

8. In World War I the Dutch and Belgians came up with some clever ideas to send messages to one another. A Belgian farmer hid them in the bodies of slaughtered pigs while another fastened them round the shaft of an arrow and shot them over the barbed-wire border. A boy flew a kite over the border and snapped the string so it carried its message safely across.

9. The most gruesome Dutch messenger was a corpse. The message was hidden beneath the body in a coffin – the German border patrol did not want to search the corpse. They even gave it a guard of honour as it took its secrets through their checkpoint.

10. One of the safest World War I message-carriers was the entertainer who performed on stage as a "memory man" – he held all the messages and secrets in his head.

Or, just as safe, was the Frenchman who wrote

F A C T F I L E

the messages on a cigarette paper, crumpled it into a ball and hid it behind his glass eye. A German border guard was not going to say, "Take out your eye!"

SET A SPY
TO CATCH A SPY

*I*ntelligence services try to gather as much information as they can about enemies of the state – people who want to cause trouble in their own country – as well as foreign enemies. Counter-intelligence services try to stop enemy agents spying on them. In Russia in 1906 the government was plagued by revolutionaries – men and women who wanted to destroy the Tsar and his royal family, then take over the country for themselves. But these revolutionaries were simply Russian students and workers by day and assassins only when they needed to be. How do you begin to look for enemies of the state when they look just like honest people? You use a spy...

Date: 1906
Place: St Petersburg, Russia

The cellar below the college was dimly lit by oil lamps. They made the stuffy room hot and smoky at the best of times. Now it was crowded with young men and women it was like a furnace. They murmured softly, and some looked nervously towards the door, waiting for the St Petersburg police to burst in and arrest them.

Ivan Aseff didn't seem to notice the heat, though the sweat ran down from his thick, dark hair and into his eyes. He sat on the platform with three men and a woman. Their clothes were shabby and their faces thin and hungry, but they didn't look like killers. Ivan rose to his feet, held up a hand and the murmuring died.

"Brothers and sisters of the Social Revolutionary Party. Welcome. A special welcome to the new members who have joined us tonight. You have come here and put your lives at risk. If the police know you belong to the party then they will shoot you." Suddenly his dark, bearded face lightened with a grin. "And if the party discover that you were sent by the police ... then we will shoot you!"

There was a nervous laugh from the students which Ivan waved away. "You are only here because at least two friends have spoken for you. Have no fear, we trust you. We know you are here because you believe in the revolution. And you know that there is only one way to win the war against the Tsar and his evil state. By violence."

There was a lot of murmuring in agreement and nodding of heads. "Kill the lot of them," a long-haired girl with wild eyes said, and several students clapped.

"We cannot kill them all," Ivan said calmly. "But we can kill their leaders. If we remove the heads of state then it will be like removing the heads of a coop full of chickens. The bodies will collapse shortly after."

"We can't get near them," cried a small man in a dust-coloured jacket. "The Secret Police protect them too well."

Ivan Aseff opened his eyes wide and spread his hands. "Then what have we got to do first, comrade?"

The little man frowned and shook his head. Then the long-haired girl shouted, "Kill Peter Stolypin, the Secret Police chief!"

That idea was greeted by more cheers. "Thank you, Comrade Olga. We must kill that villain Stolypin, then the headless Secret Police will collapse."

"Shoot him!" someone called.

"Blow up his office!"

"Bomb his car!"

The student leader held up a hand for calm. "It is clear that a large group like this cannot make a detailed plan to assassinate Stolypin. We need to form one of our assassination squads."

"Aye, a Battle Organization," the little man said.

"Exactly, Boris, a Battle Organization. A few trusted people who will make a plan and carry it out. If everyone in this room tries to plan then it will be hard to keep the secret. And, don't forget, there is always the chance that the police have planted a spy in the room."

Students looked nervously at one another and wondered if they could trust even their best friend.

"I want names!" Ivan said suddenly. "Names of people we trust to help me in this Battle Organization. If there are any doubts about any member, then vote against them and keep our secret safe."

Ten names were put forward and voted on. Many of the students named had enemies in the room and were voted out. After 20 minutes of arguing Ivan was left with only two names. Two people who were trusted by everyone. The wild-eyed Olga and the shabby Boris.

"This meeting will carry on with Nikita in charge," Ivan announced. "You will discuss ways of damaging the rail links between here and Moscow. Meanwhile, I will go and plan with Comrade Olga and Comrade Boris."

The three members of the Battle Organization left the steaming room and climbed the stairs to the college restaurant. "We are in full view of everyone here!" Olga objected.

"All the better," Ivan told her. "No one will suspect that we would meet to plot in a public place like this."

Little Boris nodded wisely. "We are just three friends sharing some tea."

"Now, comrades, you will divide this task between you. One must watch Minister Peter Stolypin carefully so we know his movements and can plot the best time and place to strike. The other must arrange for the assassination."

"I will carry out the assassination," Boris said. "I killed the Minister for Education back in 1901. I have proved myself. I deserve the honour of killing Stolypin."

"And I'll watch his movements," the girl said. "I have a disguise as a street flower-seller that lets me stand outside the government buildings."

"You will each need a team of helpers," Ivan Aseff told them. "Gather together the people that you trust the most. Then write down their names and addresses on a sheet of paper and give them to me in a week's time."

"Why?" Boris asked.

"What will you be doing?" Olga put in.

"I will be their guardian angel," Ivan said and sipped at his tea. "I have contacts inside the Secret Police ... friends of the Social Revolutionary Party. They will make sure that you and your teams are safe from arrest."

Boris frowned and wiped his nose on the sleeve of his faded jacket. "Why can't they kill Peter Stolypin themselves if they are so close to him?"

"Because they would give themselves away. They have other duties. Once Stolypin is dead we go for the blood of the Tsar himself. And *you*, Boris ... *you* can go down in history as the man who destroyed that wicked tyrant."

The little man seemed to grow a little at the thought. "Stolypin first, the Tsar next."

"Exactly," Ivan smiled. "Now, make your plans – and make those lists – then meet me here exactly seven days from now." Olga and Boris rose. "Remember," Ivan told them. "Do not do *anything* without telling me first. We need iron discipline. It is only with discipline that we will win through."

Ivan watched them go as he sat back and finished his tea. "The workers have nothing to lose but their chains," he muttered to himself. "They have a world to gain. Workers of the world, unite."

One week later he was sitting at the same table. Olga arrived first, her thin face wearing a broad grin and her coat flapping around her as she walked across the restaurant. "Calm, Olga, calm," Ivan muttered. "We never know who is watching and who is a spy for the government."

"But I have exciting news!" she said, pushing her long hair back from her pale face.

"Then you can tell Boris too – here he is now," Ivan said. "See the way he strolls across the room as if he were going to meet his tax inspector – not his fellow terrorists? Copy him, Olga, copy him."

"Yes, Comrade Ivan," she said humbly.

Boris sat at the table and took out a bundle of papers. "My lecture notes," he said. "See? Here are my notes on the history of Tsar Peter the Great." He pushed the papers across to Ivan and said in a low voice, "Take the bottom paper and put it in your pocket – do not let anyone see you do it. That is a list of the names of my bomb makers, the suppliers of the explosives and the fuses and so on."

"Very interesting!" Ivan said, then lowered his voice too. "Well done, Comrade Boris." He looked at Olga. "See how we do things in the Battle Organization? Trust no one, Olga. No one."

She leaned forward with a worried expression. "My list is in my pocket," she breathed.

"Then leave your coat over the back of the chair, fetch us some tea and I will take it out when I'm sure it is safe," Ivan said.

As she left the table the Battle Organization leader smiled at Boris. "She is willing, but still has a lot to learn. It seems she has news for us."

When the girl returned she could not wait to begin. "Minister Peter Stolypin is having an official party at his villa next Thursday."

"We would never get past the security," Ivan Aseff sighed.

"Leave that to me," Boris said. "There are ways."

"What ways are those?" his leader said stiffly. "You must do nothing without my approval."

"I and three of my best men will disguise ourselves as waiters. We will enter by the kitchens and move into the main room. We will plant bombs near where Stolypin will be sitting."

Ivan nodded slowly and asked questions about the details of the attack. "And I will see my contacts in the Secret Police and make sure one of our friends is on duty at the kitchen door." He quickly smiled at his comrades. "Well done, Olga. Well done, Boris. We will not meet again before Thursday night. It will be a glorious day for the revolution."

"The Tsar next," Boris said fiercely and his fist gripped the tea cup hard.

"The Tsar next," Ivan agreed.

The leader of the Battle Organization left the college and turned towards the city of St Petersburg. The street lighting was poor. Anyone could have been following him. They would be well hidden in the deep pools of shadow and the darkened doorways, but Ivan Aseff never looked back once. He passed the front of the bleak stone face of the government offices and turned down a narrow alley between two blocks. A yellow lamp burned dully over a doorway and he stepped inside.

A uniformed guard looked up from a desk and said, "Good evening, Aseff."

"Minister Stolypin is expecting me," the terrorist said politely. Five minutes later he was sitting in a deep cushioned chair in the minister's office. Stolypin sat next to him. He was a heavy man with several chins rolling over a starched white collar. His thick eyebrows went upwards and made him look like a startled devil.

"So, Ivan, who is the victim to be this time?"

Ivan Aseff gave a slow grin. "Actually, you are, Peter."

The minister glared at him. "That is not funny."

"The Social Revolutionary Party chose you as their chief target … I had to go along with them."

"And you had better make sure the plot does not succeed."

"It won't!" Ivan laughed. "Not with me organizing it."

The minister took a cigar from his pocket and used it to point at the terrorist. "You set up an assassination attempt on the Minister of Education," he reminded him.

"It's the best way to bring the assassins out into the open where you can arrest them. You arrested twelve members of the Social Revolutionary Party that day."

"But that assassination attempt worked! The minister died," Stolypin cried.

"Sometimes we have to pay a small price for our success," Ivan shrugged.

"You are not paying it with my life," Stolypin said, and bit hard on the cigar.

Ivan took two sheets of paper from his pocket. "Here are the names of the plotters…"

"I'll arrest them now."

"No! If you do that they'll know they've been betrayed. You must wait till Thursday evening before you have them arrested."

"Thursday evening? That's the night of the official party at my villa."

"Exactly. Wait till then. You can net all of these fish at the same time and I can go on with the next plot."

"Which is?"

"After I've failed to kill you I am going to fail to kill the Tsar!" Ivan said cheerfully. "If I am going to be any use at all, then the Battle Organization have to believe that your clever police defeated them. They must never suspect a spy in their midst."

"Hah!" the minister laughed harshly. "You are not in their midst though, are you? You're at the top!"

"The top," Ivan agreed. "That's the beauty of it. I'm at the top. The very top."

Ivan Aseff sipped tea in the restaurant at the college. Olga and Boris should be under lock and key by now, he guessed.

So he was startled to see the pale-faced girl drift across the room and sit at his table. "Olga?" he said. "What has happened?"

"A most wonderful thing," she said softly.

"What? Has Boris succeeded?"

"Boris is a hero," she said. "Who would guess that little man could be so brave?"

"He's killed Stolypin?" Ivan gasped.

"No, he's killed himself."

"Tell me exactly what happened."

"It seems the Secret Police were waiting for him and his friends at the party. But he broke free and ran into the main room where the party was being held and set off his bomb. He killed twenty-seven of the guests and even wounded Stolypin's children."

"But not Stolypin?"

"Not Stolypin."

"Thank God."

She looked at him curiously and saw something new in his sweating face. "Your friends in the Secret Police ... the ones who should have let him through ... they didn't," she said.

"Obviously."

A squad of four soldiers with rifles stopped at the door of the café and their sergeant threw it open. The girl had her back turned towards them but Ivan could see them clearly.

"Just how friendly *are* you with the Secret Police?" she asked.

The sergeant marched across the floor, his boots clattering on the bare boards.

"Very friendly," Ivan said.

"The Social Revolutionary Party will have you executed," Olga hissed as the soldier put his firm hands on her thin arms and dragged her away.

"They'll never find out," Ivan told her as she was dragged towards the door.

"I'll tell them!" she screamed.

The soldiers pulled back the bolts on their rifles and covered her with the cold steel bayonets. "No, Olga," Ivan Aseff said. "You won't be telling anyone anything. Take her away, Sergeant."

The sergeant saluted the terrorist traitor. "Yes, sir."

When it became clear that the Revolutionaries were winning the struggle against the Royalists, Ivan Aseff simply changed sides again. He joined a plot to kill the Tsar. The plot failed, but that wasn't Aseff's fault – he really had plotted to kill his old friends' leader. Within ten years the Tsar had given up his throne. A year later the Revolutionaries shot him and his family dead.

Boris's disguise as a waiter had helped him kill several of the Tsar's supporters and, for spies, disguise has always been one of their greatest weapons...

Spy Disguises

Spying is called a "cloak and dagger" business. The truth is that a spy would soon be spotted if he or she wore a cloak and carried a dagger! A spy will usually try to appear as someone harmless who has a perfect right to be where they are.

1. In 1582 an old man in a grey cloak was arrested as he crossed from Scotland into northern England. He claimed to be a dentist and had all the instruments for the job, so the border guards let him through. Luckily they kept his equipment. Their captain, Sir John Forster, examined the instruments closely and came across a coded message hidden behind the mirror. It was a letter from the French to Mary, Queen of Scots and the discovery helped the English defeat a plot against the life of Queen Elizabeth I. Mary, Queen of Scots was executed – the deadly dentist lived.

2. King Louis XV of France (1710–74) used the agent Chevalier d'Eon as a spy. They decided that d'Eon would be best disguised as a woman. Of course, he couldn't suddenly turn up as a strange woman at a meeting with foreign visitors and talk about their secrets. They would suspect and check

F
A
C
T

F
I
L
E

up on him. So he spent years dressed as a woman to make his disguise foolproof. At the end of his life he moved to London, where he kept his identity as a woman. His British friends were shocked to discover, at his funeral, that he was a man!

3. Disguises not only help spies get into secret places, they also help them to escape if they are caught. Robert Baden-Powell acted like a harmless drunk to get into German shipyards. He was soon arrested, but the guards let him go when they *smelled* him! He had soaked his clothes in brandy and they were sure he really was an innocent drunk.

4. British spies landing in France during World War II had a problem with beach landings: boot prints in the sand as they walked up the beach from their landing boats. British "Special Operations Executive" (SOE) came up with an answer. They made rubber footprints that strapped on to the boots and left footprints in the sand. Anyone seeing them would guess it was just a swimmer ... maybe. There are just two things wrong with this amazing disguise: (1) it would have been easier for agents to just take off their boots and (2) a German defender seeing the footprints may just suspect they belonged to a British Agent walking barefoot up the beach! Was it worth it?

F A C T

F I L E

5. Most people think of false beards and wigs as quick disguises for spies. Real spies know how difficult it is to make a false beard look natural and a beard that is clearly false will just attract attention. It is easier for them to simply shave off hair rather than try to add it. Cheek pads inside the mouth can change the shape of the face and some spies have even had surgery to alter their appearance – but that takes time, of course.

6. Spies wanting to take pictures of foreign buildings have often posed as tourists. They stood someone in front of their camera, but were really taking a picture of the building behind their friend. (Because the person in the picture was often someone's relative these pictures became known as "Aunt Minnies".) One spy was cycling alone in Austria before World War II. He made friends with the guards at a secret army camp. He asked the guards if he could have their picture to take home and they posed for him while he took photographs of the defences behind them!

BRUSH WITH DEATH

When war comes, spies are as valuable to a nation as soldiers. But spies don't have to be trained and paid agents. Sometimes the most unlikely people can show courage and cunning to outwit the enemy. In 1943 the German Army had occupied much of France. Some French people tried to fight them in an organization known as the "Underground" – blowing up German road and rail links, sending reports to their British allies or helping crashed pilots to escape capture. Other French men and women simply took every chance they could to make life difficult for the Germans, even though they would have been executed if they had been caught.

Date: May 1943
Place: Caen, France

"What did you do in the war, Papa?" the boy asked.

René Duchez pushed his chair back from the supper table and picked at his teeth with a grubby fingernail. "A little of this, a little of that," he said.

"Were you a soldier?" the boy asked.

"No, Jacques. The Germans took over Caen before I had a chance to join the Army."

"So, did you fight in the Underground? Michelle Simon's Papa was in the Underground. He was a fighter and they gave him a medal after the war. Did you fight with him?"

"No. I wasn't in the Underground."

"So what did you do?"

The boy's mother, Odette Duchez, came in from the kitchen to take away his plate. "He made a nuisance of himself!" she laughed.

"You smack my ear if I make a nuisance of myself," the child grumbled.

"Your father would have got a bullet behind the ear if he'd been caught," his mother said. "He was a spy, Jacques!"

The boy's eyes opened wide in wonder. "Were you really, Papa?"

Duchez spread his hands. "I did what I could."

"Tell me about it!"

"It was nothing special," the man said, pulling down the corners of his mouth, yet looking pleased at the same time.

"Come on, Duchez," his wife said. "Tell him about the time you stole the secret plans."

"Very well," the man said, and poured himself a glass of wine. "As you know, I am a decorator. Whenever I could I worked for the Germans. I hoped I could pick up bits of information once I was inside their headquarters and their camps. If I was painting a room and I overheard something, then I'd pass it on to my friends in the Café des Touristes. They had contacts in the Underground, of course."

"But tell me about the secret plans," young Jacques demanded.

"I'm coming to that," Duchez said. "It all started when I saw an advert in the town hall. The Germans wanted someone to decorate their commander's office. I went down to the camp to see the officer in charge. Mind you, it was hard to get in to see him. There were sentries on guard. Their French was poor and my German wasn't too good either. I tried to explain that I was a painter. I walked up to the side of the sentry box and pretended to paint it." Suddenly Duchez laughed.

"What's funny, Papa?"

"The sentry smacked me in the face with the back of his hand and knocked me off my feet!"

"Why did he do that?"

"Because the German leader, Adolf Hitler, used to be a house painter. The sentry thought I was making fun of their hero! Hah! The man pulled me to my feet and dragged me in to see his captain. Of course that's exactly the man I wanted to see in the first place. He spoke good French and at last I explained what I wanted. He said there were other decorators who had already offered to wallpaper the office. I guessed that the cheapest they could do it for would be 15,000 francs – I offered to do it for 12,000. It would cost me money, but it would get me right into the heart of the German organization."

"Weren't you scared, Papa?"

"Not at first. I was just an honest decorator doing work for the Germans. Then I met Major Schnedderer. He was a heavy man, completely bald, and on his cheek there was a scar he said he got in a duel. He was not a man to upset, I could see. As usual I acted like a simple French peasant, but all the time I was looking for my chance. When that chance came it was sooner, and greater, than I could have imagined. It was the next day, in fact. I took some wallpaper-pattern books into Major Schnedderer's office. He was just looking through them when he had a special parcel delivered!"

"Secret letters?" Jacques guessed.

"Maps!" his father said. "Schnedderer held them up to the window to study them and I could see they were the plans of the

German defences on the coast at Normandy. It was exactly what the British and Americans needed to know if they were going to land on the French coast and defeat the Germans! Then there was a knock at the door and Schnedderer went to answer it. The maps – those top-secret maps – were lying on the table in front of me. 'Take one! Take one!' a voice in my head was saying. But I knew that I'd be suspected if I tried to walk out with them under my jacket. I'd be searched, then tortured until I'd given the names of my contacts in the Underground. Then I'd be killed."

"Were you scared then?"

"Terrified! My shirt was stuck to my back with the sweat running down it. My mouth was as dry as if I were in a desert. My whole body was shaking. If that pile of plans were all copies of the same plan, then they might not miss one. If they were all different, then he would notice a missing one immediately. It was a gamble."

"So what did you do?" the boy breathed.

"I crossed the room. Schnedderer was at the door, talking to his secretary in the next room. If he just turned his head he would see me. I reached on to the table and laid my hands on the top plan. I looked around the room for somewhere to hide it. The chimney was no use. On a cold day they'd light the fire and discover it. But there was a heavy gold-framed mirror over the fireplace. I picked the map up and slipped it behind the mirror. I only hoped I'd have a chance to get it before a German discovered it."

"And did they?"

"Schnedderer came back into the room and chose his wallpaper at last. I said I'd be back on Monday to put the wallpaper up. 'I will have the walls cleared ready!' he said. 'No!' I said and I thought I was going to choke. 'That is something my workers do very well. They will put everything back exactly where they find it. There is no need for you to trouble yourself, Major!' And I walked out of the office. I don't know how. My legs would scarcely hold me up. I went straight to the Café des Touristes and swallowed a very large brandy, I can tell you!"

Odette sat at the table next to her husband and rested her chin on her hands. "When your father told me what he'd done, I didn't sleep. He snored his great ugly head off and I lay awake. I was just waiting for the Gestapo to knock on the door, march us out and shoot us."

"Would they have shot me?" Jacques asked.

"Probably!" his mother said. "You were just a baby, but that Schnedderer may have shot you just to teach the good French people of Caen a lesson!"

The boy shuddered. "But you got the plan, Papa."

"It wasn't that easy. I went in on the Monday morning and asked for Schnedderer. An officer called Keller said Schnedderer had been transferred! Keller was in charge now! And he was too busy sorting out his new job to have his office papered that day

... or the next day! It was going to be Wednesday before I got into the room!"

"Two more nights without sleep," Odette Duchez sighed. "You know, we had Gestapo officers living just two doors away from us. I'll swear I almost fainted every time I saw one walk past our door."

"That was nothing to the terror of walking into Keller's office that Wednesday morning," Duchez said. "After all, he could have found the map and simply waited and watched for me to collect it. As soon as he left me alone I checked that it was still there and I took it out. But that could have been part of his plan! He'd wait till I walked out and then arrest me with the map in my bag!"

"Is that what happened?"

"I worked all day in that office. I finished at five, rolled the map up and pushed it inside my jacket pocket. I said good-night to Keller. He just nodded at me. I walked down the stairs, past guards on the door. I said good-night to them. They let me leave. Then I reached the sentries at the fence. They let me walk through. I walked straight down the main street, all the time waiting for a voice to cry 'Halt!' and order me back. Or even just a bullet in the back of the head. It seemed that hundred-metre walk to the Café des Touristes was a hundred kilometres! But did I lose my nerve?"

"No, Papa."

"No. I stepped through the door and my friends were waiting for me. Deschambres, the plumber, Dumis, the mechanic and Harivel, my contact in the Underground. And at the table nearest the counter was a German soldier."

"To arrest you?" Jacques gasped.

"He could have been. He was an old soldier who often called in to the Café des Touristes when his duty was finished for the day. We thought he was a spy at first, but soon learned he was quite harmless. His army overcoat was hanging by the door and I pushed my way past it to get to the table of my friends. 'Well?' they asked. 'I have it,' I said quietly, though we knew old Albert could speak no French."

"But he would have seen you hand over the map!" Jacques said.

"He *would* have seen me hand over the map. So I *didn't*! Imagine the danger! There was a police car outside the café with two men in raincoats seated in the back. I knew they were not French police – they were German Secret State Police, the Gestapo. They could have come in at any time to search us."

"You had to get out of there quickly!" René's son said.

"It would have done no good. They could have stopped me just as easily outside!"

"So what did you do?"

"I played dominoes with my friends, of course. And I kept playing until the car with the Gestapo started up, drove slowly past the café and then disappeared out of the town."

"Then you handed over the map?"

"There was *still* old Albert inside the café, remember."

"Of course."

"Then Albert finished his drink and got up to go. I jumped to my feet, stepped across to the door and took hold of his overcoat. When he reached the coat-stand, I held up the coat and helped him to get into it. 'Danke schön,' he said – that is German for 'Thank you'. And he left! Harivel asked, 'What have you got for me? There is one more train to Paris today. I can be on it if you have important information.' And I told him, 'The *most* important information you will ever carry!' And I took the plans from inside my jacket. He was on the train to Paris and the plans were with the British inside a week."

"That was dangerous!" young Jacques said. "What if the Gestapo had come into the café and searched you?"

René Duchez grinned and looked at his wife. "If they had searched me from head to toe they would have found absolutely nothing!"

"Was it magic?" Jacques asked.

"No."

"Were they hidden under the table?"

"No."

"Then what did you do with them?" the boy cried.

"What would *you* have done with them?" his father asked.

"Stop teasing him and tell the lad," Odette said.

René Duchez sat back in his chair and took a long drink of the red wine. "I hid them in the only safe place in the whole café. I hid them in the overcoat pocket of old Albert, the German soldier!"

"You didn't!"

"As I entered the café I'd seen the Gestapo car and I didn't want to be caught with the plans. I certainly didn't want to pass them over to Harivel for *him* to get caught. I slipped them into the soldier's coat when it was hanging on the coat-stand. As soon as he got up to go I grabbed the coat and took them out again. *He* thought I was being a gentleman. I knew I was helping to defeat him and his invaders."

Jacques eyes were glowing. "Wait till I tell Michelle Simon! My father is a hero!"

"Germany isn't the only country to have a house painter for a hero," René shrugged.

"Did you get a medal, Papa?"

"No, my son. But when the war was over we had a great celebration in the town hall. The fighting men of the Underground were honoured – and it was only right that they should be. But when the speeches were all over and the cheering had died down, the mayor came over to me and spoke to me. 'We will never forget the part you played, René,' he said."

Madame Duchez poked him sharply in the shoulder and said, "Tell Jacques what else the mayor said to you."

"The mayor said, 'René, there is no doubt about your madness ... and there is no doubt about your courage.'"

"You see, Jacques?" Odette Duchez said as she put an arm around her husband's shoulders and squeezed. "You don't have to be a soldier with a medal to be a hero."

The secret plans that Duchez stole were vital for British and American forces when they landed on the French coast in 1944. They knew where the German defences were strong and where they were weak. They let false information reach the German defenders. It said that the British and Americans would land in one place when in fact they planned to land in another. Spies need to use such tricks to confuse an enemy...

F
A
C
T

F
I
L
E

Spy Tricks

1. Before the British and Americans landed in Italy they "accidentally" lost a secret message that showed plans to attack through Greece and Sardinia. (The truth is they meant to go through Sicily.) The secret message was planted on a dead body and dropped into the Mediterranean Sea for the Germans to find. The corpse was given a completely fake identity, as "Major Martin". His pockets held bills, theatre tickets and love-letters – all faked – as well as the secret plans for the phoney Greece plan. The Germans fell for the trick and rushed to defend Greece while their enemies landed in Sicily. The real name of the dead man is still a secret – he is simply known as "the man who never was".

2. The "man who never was" story is famous. Not so many people know that a similar idea had been tried in World War I. A British officer rode past Turkish defences and was fired at. He dropped the haversack he was carrying and appeared to have been hit. He tried to go back for it but was driven off by rifle fire and the Turks captured the bag. It was soaked in fresh blood and had a British plan of attack inside. The British let the Turks overhear

F A C T

radio messages saying how desperate they were to get the sack safely returned. Of course the plans were false and the blood was from a slaughtered pig, but the trick worked and sent the Turk defenders in the wrong direction.

3. If a spy is captured then it is vital that messages should be destroyed. British spy, Robert Baden-Powell, was held in an Austrian jail when the local police suspected him of spying. While they waited for their intelligence agents to arrive, they kindly allowed Baden-Powell to roll some cigarettes and smoke them. Of course his spy notes were written on the cigarette papers and he destroyed them. (Baden-Powell described this trick in a popular book he wrote. Later spies, who were foolish enough to try the same thing, were usually caught and often executed. Smoking can damage your health!)

4. During World War II spies were dropped into enemy countries by parachute and then had to

F I L E

F A C T

F I L E

bury the parachutes. But the German airforce sometimes dropped empty parachutes to make the British think there were spies everywhere and to waste police and Home Guard time in looking for them.

5. Spies who want to pass on messages need a "letter-box" – not a hole in somebody's door, but simply a safe place to leave a message for a partner to collect. A "live letter-box" is a person who will hold the message for you and a "dead letter-box" (or a "dead drop") is just an agreed place. A dead letter-box can be a hollow tree, a hole in the ground or the boot of a parked car. Anywhere that a message can be hidden, in fact.

6. During World War II, the Germans took over a cottage owned by an old French woman. Their maps were all over the walls but were guarded, even at night. The old woman contacted the local Resistance agent and told him to come with a camera. She gave the guard coffee full of herbs that gave him diarrhoea. Every time the guard trotted off to the toilet at the bottom of the garden, the agent slipped in and photographed the maps!

THE APPLE SPY

By the start of World War II, the Scots found they agreed with the English over one matter; they didn't like Mr Hitler and his Nazi bully boys. They fought shoulder to shoulder with their old enemy to defeat the new enemy, Germany.

Everyone remembers the "Blitz" over London. But Scotland produced a lot of warships and weapons, so she got her share of German bombs.

Scotland was also a good place to land a German spy. There were miles of deserted coastline where secret agents could be landed without being spotted. In September 1940 a group of three almost got away with it. The sharp wits of a few Scots – and a bit of luck – saved Britain from danger...

Date: September 1940
Place: Portgordon and Edinburgh, Scotland

Detective Superintendent William Merrilees stood with his back to a map of Edinburgh and spoke quietly but quickly to the men and women crowded into the room. "Two foreigners arrived at Portgordon railway station at 7:30 this morning, a man and a woman. Stationmaster John Donald became suspicious when the woman asked the name of the station. Of course, all signs have been taken down because of the war. The man pointed to the timetable on the wall and asked for two tickets to Forres. The stationmaster noticed that the man's wallet was crammed with English pound notes. He also noticed that the bottom of the man's trousers were soaked and so were the woman's stockings. He told porter John Geddes to keep the couple talking while he telephoned Constable Grieve at the local police station."

The uniformed police in the room looked grim. Constable Nixon, who always fancied himself as the Sherlock Holmes of the Lothian and Borders Police Force, turned to Policewoman Ellen Johnston on his left. "Holiday-makers, mark my words," he murmured. "Caught by the tide."

"Really?" she gasped, wide-eyed. "What would they be doing on the north-east coast?"

"Fishing," Constable Nixon said with a wise wink.

Superintendent Merrilees went on, "They were, of course, spies."

Constable Nixon coughed quietly. "I thought so. Spies pretending to be holiday-makers."

Merrilees went on, "Constable Grieve ran from his office to the railway station and asked to see the couple's identity papers. The man and woman claimed to be refugees, but their papers had no stamp to show where they had entered Britain. And both cards were in a continental style of handwriting."

"Tut! Tut! Tut!" Nixon clucked. "I'd have spotted that at once."

"Grieve phoned his superintendent at Buckie and the couple were searched. Apart from over £300 in banknotes, they were carrying a Mauser pistol and ammunition, a wireless transmitter and a code book. But the real give-away was the piece of German sausage they were carrying. No one has been able to buy such a sausage in Scotland since the war started."

"Never liked the stuff much anyway," Nixon sniffed.

"A close search in the Portgordon and Buckie area revealed that a third spy had taken a train to Edinburgh. He arrived here at 4:30 this afternoon."

There was a stir of excitement among the police in the room. Nixon looked at his watch. "Forty-five minutes ago. He could be anywhere by now."

"We'll comb the city," Superintendent Merrilees ordered and began to give tasks to small teams of men and women. Some were to try the hotels, others were to look in the cinemas, and a large group was to search the railway yards near the station. He looked at Nixon and Policewoman Ellen Johnston. "You two can come with me."

Nixon inflated his chest. "That's because we're the cream," he smiled.

"No," the superintendent frowned. "I was just thinking that if the German shot you, then Edinburgh Police wouldn't be losing much!"

"What?"

"A joke, Nixon. Just my little joke. Now, let's get down to the station and see what we can find out."

The three officers arrived at the great gloomy Waverley Station and marched to the stationmaster's office. A shrivelled old porter stood there, twisting his battered cap between his fingers. "You're McGregor?" Superintendent Merrilees asked.

"Yes, sir."

"And you helped this foreign gentleman when he stepped off the Aberdeen train?"

"I did, sir."

"Tell us exactly what happened."

"He stepped down with his case and asked if this was Edinburgh. I said, 'Well it's not New York!' He didn't laugh. He just asked where he'd get the London train and I said Platform 6. Then he asked what time, and I said 10:00 p.m. tonight. He looked a bit upset at that."

"He left the station, did he?"

"Aye, sir. Headed up to Princes Street."

"In a brown overcoat and black felt hat. Age about thirty you said?"

"That's right, sir."

Merrilees shook his head. "He'll be hard to spot in the crowds."

"What about the case?" Policewoman Johnston asked quietly.

The superintendent clicked his fingers. "Good thought, Johnston. What sort of case was he carrying?"

"He wasn't," McGregor said.

"You told us he stepped off the train with a case," Merrilees said sharply.

The old porter looked sly. "I *did*. But he put it in the Left Luggage office, didn't he!"

"Why didn't you say so?" the police chief snapped.

"You never asked."

Two minutes later the three officers were examining a large suitcase. "Do you think this is the one?" Merrilees asked.

"There's a white stain on it," Policewoman Johnston pointed out. "Probably sea water."

The senior officer looked at her with admiration. "Well done, Ellen. I'm glad we brought you along."

"I noticed that stain," PC Nixon whispered to the policewoman.

"Let's just force it open, shall we? Here we go ... what have we here?"

"A radio, sir," Nixon said quickly before Ellen could identify the metal box with dials.

"A *German* radio, Nixon. Very important. And two apples! We know what they'll be for."

"To eat?" Nixon nodded wisely.

"But you see what's missing?" the superintendent asked.

"A gun, sir," Ellen Johnston said.

"That's good!" Constable Nixon said brightly.

"That's bad, Nixon," Merrilees said with a shake of the head.

"Very *bad*," the policewoman agreed.

Nixon looked at her blankly. She explained. "He's sure to have a gun, but he must have it with him. That makes it dangerous for anyone who tries to arrest him."

The constable swallowed hard. "Yes. I was thinking that."

His senior officer slapped him on the back. "Sorry, Nixon, I know you'd like the glory of the arrest yourself. But it's so risky I just can't ask another man to do it. I'll arrest him myself."

Constable Nixon breathed out slowly. "If you insist, sir."

"Never mind," Ellen said squeezing his arm. "You'll have your chance to show your bravery another day."

"I will," the policeman nodded.

They laid their plan carefully and by eight o'clock they were in position. Superintendent Merrilees was dressed in a porter's uniform and standing behind the desk of the Left Luggage office. Constables Nixon and Johnston stood in the shadows. The evening grew darker and there were only a few dim lights in the station, and none in the blacked-out city outside. The smoke of the trains smelled sharp and stung their nostrils. Trapped in the canopy of the station it formed a thin, sooty mist.

Nine o'clock rang on the clock of the Balmoral Hotel and a man in a black hat walked quickly up to the Left Luggage counter. "Evening, sir!" Merrilees said brightly.

The man didn't reply but pushed a slip of paper over the counter.

"Number two-seven-three, sir?" the police officer said. He brought the case to the counter and noticed that the stranger kept his right hand in his pocket. "Hang on a moment, sir, and I'll bring it round the counter to you."

He raised a flap in the counter and heaved the case through. The stranger reached out a left hand but kept his right hand in his pocket. "Here, sir, I'll call a porter for you," the superintendent said quickly. He looked across the dim alley that led to the platforms and shouted, "Nixon!"

The stranger turned away, as Merrilees knew he would. In an instant the superintendent let go of the case and grabbed the man's right arm. The stranger struggled but Nixon was running towards them with Policewoman Johnston. Together they forced the hand out of the overcoat pocket and saw the man was indeed holding a gun.

"I arrest you on suspicion of espionage against His Majesty King George's government," Nixon said with a wide grin to Ellen Johnston.

She nodded with satisfaction.

That evening they were in the canteen at the central police station telling the story of the spy for the 20th time. Each time the struggle was longer and Nixon's heroism greater.

A message arrived at the table where they were drinking tea. "The prisoner is asking to speak to the brave officer that arrested him."

Nixon rose to his feet. "I guess he's ready to confess. He knows he's met his match with me."

"Can I come with you?" Ellen Johnston asked.

"Of course you can, Ellen. See a bit of good policing in action."

They walked through the police station, down the shabby green corridors until they came to the cell that held the man. The prisoner clutched at the bars, his dark eyes staring and pleading. "My apples," he said. "You have my apples?"

"I have," Nixon said.

"May I have them. Please?"

"I came to hear you confess, not to run errands for you."

"Ah!" the man nodded. "Fetch my apples and I will tell you everything. The codes, the drop-off points, the names of agents already in your country. The whole of the German spy network. Anything."

Nixon could see his name in the newspaper headlines. "I'll get a notepad and pencil."

"And the apples?"

"And the apples."

The spy gave a slow smile. "I knew you would help me."

Nixon turned and walked back towards the main office. "I wonder where we can find two wrinkled apples at this time of night?" Ellen asked.

"What for?"

"To give him," Ellen said.

"Give him his own apples," Nixon shrugged. "Can't be any harm in that." He reached into the suitcase and took the fruit out.

The policewoman's eyes opened wide. "Oh, but you can't do that!"

Nixon frowned. "Why not?"

"Because they're sure to be poisoned. One bite and he'll be dead. You won't get a word out of him. In fact, you'll be in dead trouble!"

The constable felt suddenly faint and dropped the apples on to the top of a desk. He wiped his hands on his trousers. "Poisoned?"

"Poisoned. All spies carry poison with them."

He cleared his throat. "Yes, well spotted, Policewoman Johnston. I wondered how long it would take you to work that out. I knew it all along."

"Of course you did, Constable Nixon," she smiled. "Of course you did. As long as we have policemen like you, the Germans will never defeat us."

The constable poked at the apples with a finger. "Hah! Apples! The oldest trick in the book. Never fooled me for a minute."

He turned and collected his helmet from a rack on the wall. Only Ellen Johnston noticed that his hands were trembling as he put it on.

The three spies were taken to London for questioning and tried at the Old Bailey. All three were found guilty. The Edinburgh spy and the man caught at Portgordon were hanged. The woman was pardoned, even though it was clear she was the leader. It seems she agreed to betray her German masters and work for the British Secret Service.

She said that the three spies landed in a seaplane then rowed ashore in a dinghy. Three bicycles were lowered into the dinghy but dropped into the sea. The spies had expected to cycle 600 miles to London! If it hadn't been for the accident with the cycles, and the sharp-witted people of Portgordon and Buckie, Britain could have been in great danger. (Though a World War I spy arrived in England with his cycle and was arrested before he had ridden a quarter of a mile – he was riding on the right-hand side of the road as he always did in Germany!)

The clever Portgordon stationmaster, John Donald, was made an MBE, while Superintendent William Merrilees went on to be Chief Constable of the Lothian and Borders Police Force.

The Germans were betrayed by the radio they carried. Many spies need special equipment...

F A C T F I L E

Spy Equipment

The American spy organization, the Central Intelligence Agency (CIA), nicknames spy gadgets as "sneakies". But these have been around longer than the CIA.

1. **Secret compartments.** Hiding messages, plans and equipment from the enemy needs some careful planning. A messenger from Charles I's queen was captured by Oliver Cromwell in the English Civil War. He was stripped and searched but no message was found. It was only when Cromwell ordered his saddle to be torn apart that the vital letter was found.

2. **Secret pockets.** In the 1890s a British officer spying on a demonstration of a new exploding bullet in France had a secret pocket in the long tail of his coat. He popped the shell case into the pocket – sadly the metal was still hot and his coat-tails began to smoke and gave the game away!

3. **Maps.** Spies in World War II needed maps, but they would be shot if they were caught with one in their pocket. So maps were cut into 52 pieces and each piece sandwiched into a playing card. When

F
A
C
T

F
I
L
E

the agent was safely out of sight, he or she could peel off the face of the card and put the 52 pieces together to assemble the map again.

4. **Bugs.** Spies who want to listen in on enemy meetings will try to leave a microphone and transmitter in the meeting place – a "bug". These bugs are so small they can be hidden in a watch or a pen. The latest ones are just 4 mm thick and the size of a credit card, so they can be easily hidden in a diary or a pocket calculator.

5. **Cameras.** Spies have wanted to photograph documents, enemy agents and secret defences ever since the camera was invented in the 1840s. By the 1880s there were cameras designed to fit into hats, ties and books. By 1948 a camera could be fitted into a wrist-watch. Modern video cameras can spy through a hole the size of a pinhead.

6. **Guns.** Guns need to be well hidden and Secret Service scientists have come up with many clever ones – pens and pencils that fire a shot, a ring that hid a five-shot revolver and a glove that held a single-shot pistol. Even a harmless-looking umbrella has had a gas-injector in the tip that fired a poison pellet into the victim. A Bulgarian, Georgi Markov, died from a poison umbrella shot when walking in a London street in 1978.

7. **Knives.** These can take the form of sharpened coins and special blades built into the heel of a shoe. This is useful if the agent is tied up and needs to cut himself or herself free.

8. **Bombs.** A German scientist called Scheele invented a fire-bomb for use by agents in World War I. The lead tube, the size of a cigar, had two compartments separated by a thin piece of copper. One compartment held sulphuric acid and the other picric acid. The sulphuric acid ate through the copper in a few days and let the two acids mix; this created a fierce flame. If the "cigar bomb" was slipped into a bale of material or a sack of grain before it was loaded on to a ship, then a fire would start when the ship was at sea and destroy it. Dr Scheele also invented a fire-bomb that looked like a lump of coal and would never be noticed on a coal ship – till it went off, of course.

FACT FILE

9. **Poison pills.** Many spies in World War II were given small poison pills. If they were captured then they could crush the pill between their teeth, swallow the poison and die. This would save them from being tortured and betraying their friends. Several German spies used the poison pills but there's no record of a British spy ever using one. A German spy called Hermann Goertz was imprisoned in Ireland for spying. At the end of the war he was released and ordered to return to Germany. He believed Germany was still run by the Nazis and he'd be shot when he landed, so he took the poison and killed himself. In fact he would have been perfectly safe.

10. **Poison gases.** Spies in films seem to have supplies of special gases – one squirt in the face and an enemy is dead. In fact, such gases do exist and no doctor could tell how the victim has died – with a tiny amount you can commit the perfect murder. British and American agents say that the gas, known as FEA, has already been used by the Russians to put "problem" people out of the way.

XX SPELLS
"DOUBLE CROSS"

What would you do if you were a spy and you were caught? The American spy Nathan Hale was captured by the British and told he would be executed. "I'm sorry that I have only the one life to give for my country," he said. He was hanged and became an American hero.

Before the start of World War I in 1914, spies tried to behave like gentlemen. When Colonel Alfred Redl betrayed Austria to the Russians and was caught in 1913, he asked his captors if he could have a few minutes alone. They agreed, even though they knew what he planned to do – he went to his room and shot himself. Were all spies that determined to die for their country?

Date: 17 September 1940
Place: Cambridge, England

Call me a coward and a traitor if you like. But I did not want to die for Germany! So why did I agree to spy for them back in 1939, you ask? For the excitement. For the *adventure.* And because it was better than being in the Army with all that parading and marching and hard work.

I couldn't face joining the German Army when the war started. I didn't fancy being shouted at by some red-faced, foul-mouthed sergeant. So, when the German Military Intelligence officer came to me in September 1939, I jumped at the chance to spy for them. Hah! Jumped at the chance. That's a joke! I really *did* jump – out of a plane on my first and last spying mission.

"You speak good English," the Intelligence officer said.

"I've travelled around the world," I admitted.

"We need men like you, Wulf Schmidt, to spy for us. We would train you, of course."

And the training took a year. Learning how to operate a radio, the codes I'd need and my cover story. The story was that I was Harry Williamson from Denmark – that was easy enough for me because I was born on the border with Denmark and I knew it well.

The truth was I was Agent A3725.

Then I was told I'd be sent to England to spy on their defences and their war plans. "Where will I be landed?" I asked.

"Cambridgeshire," my German instructor told me.

I laughed. "How will a submarine drop me in Cambridgeshire?"

"You are not going by submarine," he said. He was not laughing. "You will be dropped by parachute."

Have you ever jumped into a cold swimming pool and felt the shock? That was how the news chilled me. "I'm scared of heights!" I said.

"You'll be on the ground in no time," he snapped.

"That's what terrifies me!" I said.

"We drop agents on moonless nights, so you won't even see the ground."

"How will I know when I'm there?"

"You'll know," he said and he gave a yellow-toothed grin. He was enjoying this.

The parachute training was a nightmare. Sitting in the doorway at 10,000 feet and waiting to jump made me sick.

Vomiting at 300 kilometres per hour is not funny. At least I wasn't afraid of being caught as a spy. "I'm not worried about what the British will do to me," I wrote and told my mother. "The parachute drop will kill me before they even get their hands on me!"

The night of the landing, 17 September 1940, was *not* as bad as I had feared – it was at least ten times *worse*. "There's a full moon!" I cried. "What happened to the idea of dropping me in the dark?"

"The bombers can see the British cities better on a moonlit night."

"I'm going to spy on them, not bomb them," I sighed.

"Your plane will cross the English Channel with a squadron of bombers. That way they won't spot it."

The Cambridgeshire countryside was silver-green with black shadows of hedgerows and bright ribbons of road. It was quite beautiful. It was also a long way down. I sat in the open door. "Go!" the navigator called.

At that moment the plane rocked and I was thrown against the door frame. My watch strap caught in the door latch and was ripped off my wrist. It had been a present from my mother. It spun down towards the English soil and I followed it moments later. My hand was damaged too, but I hadn't time to worry about it then. The parachute snapped open and the jerk seemed to squeeze the air from my lungs. The cold wind stung my eyes to tears and by the time I had cleared them I saw the ground was rushing towards me. Luckily, the field was soft and muddy so I managed to land without breaking my neck.

I lay on the ground and groaned for five minutes. In training they said I had to move quickly after I landed. But the trainers weren't there. I dragged myself to a ditch at the edge of the field and buried my flying suit and parachute as well as I could with my one good hand. Then I picked up my suitcase and limped on to the road.

I had seen a cluster of houses just before I dropped and set off in what seemed the right direction. For once I was in luck. The village was there, quiet in the moonlight. The village sign had been removed so that German spies would not know where they had landed. That wasn't very sporting.

I walked to the middle of the green. No lights showed from the blacked-out windows and no one was on the streets at this late hour. I soaked my throbbing hand under the village pump and then rested my back against it. After all the tension, and a week of sleepless nights, I fell asleep. It may sound amazing, but I slept soundly under the village pump until morning.

When I woke, people were passing me in the street and looking at me with suspicion. I jumped to my feet, grabbed my suitcase and brushed the creases from my suit. "Good morning!"

I called to a boy with a school-bag on his back. His eyes opened wide as saucers before he turned and ran.

Then two old men in khaki battledress uniforms shuffled towards me with ancient rifles pointing at me. The lettering on their shoulders said LDV – Local Defence Volunteers by name, but better known to the English as Dad's Army.

"Raise your hands!" one croaked. He looked more afraid than I was.

"I am a Danish businessman," I began.

"And I'm Winston Churchill," his friend sneered.

I stretched out a hand. "Pleased to meet you, Mr Churchill!" I said. He jumped back as if my hand held a gun.

"I think you had better come with us," the first one said.

My career as a spy had lasted a few hours and would last just a few hours more, I guessed. I hoped they would shoot me quickly. I couldn't face being tortured. I had already decided that if they started pushing splinters of wood up my fingernails I would talk.

The cell I was locked in was comfortable enough. The policeman in charge was even friendly. "The gentlemen from Military Intelligence will be with you in half an hour," he smiled. "Here's a cup of tea and some toast. Bet it's better than the stuff they feed you in Germany."

"I'm from Denmark!" I said.

He raised one eyebrow and laughed. "Oh yes? And I'm Winston Churchill."

"So! There are two of you in one village!" I sighed. "Amazing!"

"What's that?"

"Nothing, just my little joke."

The man who arrived to question me was small, round-faced and wearing wire-rimmed glasses. He came into the cell smoking a pipe and offered me a cigarette. "Good morning, A3725. Welcome to England!" he said.

"I am a Danish citizen," I said. "The Danish are your friends. Why do you lock me away like this?"

"You are Agent A3725 and we've been expecting you," he said and sat down with a brown folder full of papers. "Let's see," he said taking a paper out. "Two of your men landed here six months ago and your job is to make contact with them."

"I am a Danish citizen," I said.

I waited for him to tell me he was Winston Churchill too! But he just shook his head sadly. "The game's up, Wulf Schmidt."

"My name is Harry Williamson."

"Your name is Wulf Schmidt and you are here to collect information on the British war effort." He was very calm about it.

"You will torture me?" I asked.

He looked shocked. "Good lord, no! Nothing so messy as that!"

"You will shoot me, then?"

"Not unless I have to," he said with a shrug. "You are much more useful to us alive."

"Useful? To you? In what way?"

"You can send messages back to your masters in Germany."

"What sort of messages?"

"The information that they want, of course. Your two friends are already doing it for us. We caught them when they landed six months ago and they're working for us now. That's how we know all about you," he explained. "They didn't want to be shot, you see. Do you?"

"No!" I said quickly. "But I don't understand why you want me to send your secrets back to Germany."

"Because you will be telling the Germans everything we want them to know."

"Lies?"

"Not all of them." He took off his glasses and polished them on a huge white handkerchief. "The information is put together by a special committee called Committee 20. Now, as you know, '20' in Roman numerals is XX. It's a little joke among us – we call it 'Double Cross'. Get it? XX – double-cross."

"Very funny," I said, but I didn't laugh.

"You're right," he sighed. "Not one of the best jokes in the world. But the fact is, that's what we want *you* to do. Double-cross your German masters. We'll pay you well, look after you ... and let you live. All you have to do is feed Committee 20 information to your old friends."

"I see," I nodded. "This information will mislead the German Army?"

"Exactly!" he chuckled. "And they will ask you to find certain pieces of information that will prove useful to us."

"What do you mean?"

He leaned forward. "They may ask you to take a trip north and report on anti-aircraft guns in Newcastle. What does that tell us?"

"That they are planning to bomb Newcastle?" I guessed.

"Exactly! Sometimes you will say the British have no guns there when we will really have extra ones in place. We'll blow the Luftwaffe out of the sky. Other times you will say there are a thousand guns and planes defending the place, when there aren't ... that way they may simply leave us alone. You see the way it works?"

"I see."

"Now, old chap. Do you fancy working for us? Or shall I just take you out into the yard and put a bullet in the back of your head?" he asked. He was like a kindly schoolmaster asking if I wanted to choose between playing soccer or rugby!

What do you think I said? What would *you* have said to an offer like that? Of course I said, "Yes."

"Then you will need a code-name. What is it to be?" he asked and seemed to be enjoying himself.

"I called myself Harry Williamson," I told him.

"You know," he said, "we have a comedian who is very popular in Britain. They call him Harry, too. Harry Tate. That's what we'll call you … Tate!"

So, for the next five years my friends called me Wulf, and my employers called me Tate. I was one of the best agents the Germans had in Britain. I blew up more bridges and arms factories than the Luftwaffe bombs … at least that's what my reports said.

Adolf Hitler himself was impressed by my work. In fact, the German High Command believed I was such a German hero they awarded me the Iron Cross (second class and first class), their highest honours. Their radio message went on to say, "The crosses will be presented to your brother until the day you return to Germany after we have won the war."

Of course, Germany lost the war. Every single spy landed in Britain had been captured. The brave ones refused to work with the British and they were shot. But 120 of them, including me, were "turned" and used against our homeland. No wonder Germany lost the war. Every piece of spy information they received was sent by their enemy.

I couldn't keep the Iron Crosses, of course. But I did go back to my home to collect them from my brother. I went through the blackened rubble of all those ruined German towns and knew that I was in some way to blame. You have to remember, though, I had also seen the fire-storms that lit up London and the Blitz that shattered so many other British towns.

Call me a traitor, but don't blame me. Blame war.

I became a spy because I wanted excitement. I returned from the ruins of Germany with my Iron Crosses and I had had a bellyful of excitement. Enough to last me a lifetime.

The British were good to me. They said I could keep on working for them. Their old allies, the Russians, were building a wall of secrecy to keep the British and Americans out – an "Iron Curtain" Winston Churchill called it. They said I could go back to Germany to spy on the Russians. I said, "Thank you – but no." Still, the British let me stay.

I took a job as a newspaper photographer and the most excitement I've had since is a big wedding!

And somewhere, filed away and forgotten in a British Military Intelligence office, there are two of the most curious souvenirs ever to be held by one of their agents. Two German Iron Crosses for gallantry. If you will excuse the bad joke – a sort of double-cross!

Wulf Schmidt kept his wartime secret for 50 years. In 1990, a television programme was made about Committee 20 and Wulf described his work. His friends and family were astonished to learn of his spy past.

The XX plan worked perfectly and the Germans never knew that their spies had died or switched sides. They continued to send messages in code, but as the British knew all their codes they may as well have sent them in clear English!

From the earliest times, spies have tried to disguise their messages so that they stayed secret even if an enemy came across them...

F
A
C
T

F
I
L
E

Spy Codes

There is always a danger that an enemy will find your message. If they do then it is probably important that they can't make any sense of it. Or at least it will slow them down. (An Arab in the 1600s decoded a message to the Sultan of Morocco, but it took him 16 years!) Since the earliest days of spying, agents have used "codes".

1. The first code-makers we know about were the Chinese of 1000 BC. Army commanders learned 40 lines of a poem. Each line meant something different. If they sent line 17, say, then it might mean, "Please send more arrows", or line 32 might mean, "I have defeated an enemy attack". The line of the poem was then included in an ordinary report so it would be impossible for an enemy to understand.

2. Alexander the Great could read his enemies' letters because they didn't use a code. He was much more careful. He wrote messages on a strip of paper spiralled round a stick. When the paper was unwound the letters were scrambled. A reader with the right sized stick could wind the paper round it and see the message again.

F
A
C
T

3. A hundred years later the Greek writer, Polybius (203–120 BC), came up with the number square. Twenty-five letters of the alphabet were arranged into five rows of five columns.

	1	2	3	4	5
1	G	Q	B	T	O
2	D	N	L	X	J
3	R	A	W	F	Y/Z
4	E	V	P	S	I
5	K	U	M	C	H

So "A" is 2 across – 3 down, or 23. "B" is 31 and "D" is 12. So 31-23-12 spells "bad".

Amazingly this type of code was still being used by the French Resistance in World War II, 2,000 years later.

4. Julius Caesar used the simple trick of moving all the letters of the alphabet three spaces along. If he wanted to write ABCDE then his code said DEFGH. It is still known as the "Caesar Alphabet".

5. Mary, Queen of Scots sent and received messages in prison that were hidden in beer barrels. To be extra safe, she wrote letters to her agents in a code that was a mixture of Greek letters and shapes. The English spy-master, Sir Francis Walsingham, had spies who copied every letter in the barrels before they were replaced and passed on. He had a code-breaker called Thomas

F
I
L
E

Phelippes who broke the code easily. Mary's agents were arrested and died horribly, half-hanged, then cut apart before being beheaded. Mary herself was beheaded shortly afterwards. All because her code was cracked.

6. In World War I, Britain and France were struggling against the German Army. President Woodrow Wilson and the American people did not want to get mixed up in the battles in Europe. Then the Germans sent a coded message to their agent in Mexico. It told the Mexicans that if they invaded America from the south, then Germany would help them. The British spy-master Reginald Hall (nicknamed "Blinker" Hall because of his habit of blinking) got a copy of the message. His code-cracking expert, Reverend William Montgomery, was a schoolteacher interested in puzzles. He decoded the German message. The American people were so furious when they read the decoded message they changed their minds and America joined the war. That one broken code probably changed the course of history.

7. Two Dutch sailors in Portsmouth spied for Germany in World War I. Instead of sending a code of scrambled letters they posed as cigar salesmen and sent orders openly through the telegraph system. "1,000 Havana cigars" meant *one battleship* had arrived in Portsmouth harbour – "2,000 Corona cigars" meant two cruisers were in port. It seemed a perfect system. But a Post Office

F
A
C
T

F
I
L
E

clerk noticed the size of the orders which were adding up to almost 5,000 cigars a day. The whole of Portsmouth couldn't smoke that many. British Military Intelligence Department 5 (MI5) arrested the men.

8. A French woman was able to send messages to spies across the valley from her house, using her washing line. She hung out garments that spelled out the message. Her ABC used the English language to confuse the Germans even further and it read as follows: Apron, Blouse, Collar, Duster, Eiderdown, Frock, Gloves, Handkerchief, Jacket, Knickers, Lace, Mat, Nightdress, Overall, Pants, Quilt, Roller-towel, Skirt, Trousers, Undershirt, Vest, Waistcoat, Yoke.

9. A World War II US general at army headquarters didn't bother sending orders in code. Instead he told a Navaho Indian on his staff the message. The Native American passed the message on to one of his tribe in the battalion who changed it back into the English instructions for the fighting men. Apart from the Navahos, there were just 28 people in the world who spoke the language – and none of them was German. In the 1960s, Irish troops fighting for the United Nations in the Congo spoke to one another in their native Gaelic – quite sure that no African spies could understand a word.

10. The German code machine called Enigma was so good at scrambling messages they believed it

F
A
C
T

F
I
L
E

was completely safe. In fact, one of the workers in a factory that made the Enigma machine gave the secret to the British. British experts then invented a very early sort of computer to decode Enigma messages and were able to read some of Germany's greatest war secrets. The Germans didn't know that their Enigma code system had been cracked and the British told no one until 25 years after the war had ended.

ARMCHAIR AGENT

WARNING
UNAUTHORIZED ACCESS TO THESE
FILES IS PROHIBITED UNDER
FEDERAL LAW

Spies have always used the latest inventions to keep ahead of the enemy: when cameras were invented, spies had miniature ones made; when radio came along, they were glad of a new way of reporting back to headquarters; aeroplanes became spy-planes and satellites became their eyes in the sky. At the beginning of the twenty-first century computers hold the world's secrets. Will spies turn to using computers to search out secrets? Of course they will. What's more, they already have been for some years. Spying by computer may seem clean and safe compared to the ways of the old agents. One of the first cases to be uncovered was in Germany – it turned out to be anything but safe for one of the new breed of young spies...

Date: Autumn/winter 1989
Place: Hanover, Germany

Karl was my friend but now Karl is dead. They said he was a spy and that's why he's dead. But it wasn't that simple.

I was 14 years old in 1986. Most boys in my class were interested in football – a few were interested in girls. I was only interested in computers. They called me a freak, but I didn't care.

I was an only child and a lonely child. But through my computer I met all the friends I wanted. Every night after school

I raced through my homework, then sat at my computer screen for four hours or more. A small box at the side of the machine was connected to the phone line and through the phone lines I could exchange messages with friends at the other side of the world.

But Karl was my special computer friend, and now Karl is dead.

I first realized that Karl was local when I switched on my computer one evening in the autumn of 1988 and found an electronic message waiting for me. "Interested in making money from your computer? Contact Karl." And it gave his electronic address. I saw that it was local and I knew I needed money desperately to keep my computer up to date.

I tapped in his address and contacted Karl. At first we exchanged harmless messages and then one evening Karl's message asked, "Why not call round and see me?"

I had contacted hundreds of people over the computer network; I'd never met one face-to-face. Karl's address was just on the other side of Hanover – the side where the wealthy people lived. It was just 20 minutes on a bus. I switched off my computer early that night and left the house.

Karl lived in a flat with security doors at the main entrance. I'd never come across anything like it and pushed nervously at the button marked "Karl Koch".

"Who's there?" asked a tinny voice from the speaker.

"Peter. Peter Ahlen," I said. A buzz sounded from the lock on the door and I pushed it open. I took the lift to the third floor and found him waiting at the door. I guessed he was about 25 years old. He was thin and pale, like someone who never saw the sun. He wore round spectacles in wire frames and the eyes behind the glass were never still. We shook hands awkwardly.

"I guess you'll want to see my set-up," he said.

I nodded shyly and he led me through the living-room and into a small room that was lit mainly by the blue-green light from his computer screen. The computer simply amazed me. If I was Aladdin with three wishes I'd have wished for a computer like that. "Show me what you can do," he said.

I hadn't realized I was there for some kind of test, but I sat at the keyboard and found some of my favourite network sites in the USA and Britain. He looked faintly disappointed. "Are you into hacking?"

I took a deep breath. Using the network to steal files from other people's programs is illegal. I knew how to do it – I'd simply never dared. "No," I said, a little ashamed that he'd see me as some sort of wimp.

That night he showed me how to hack – really hack. How to get into secret files by discovering their passwords and reading documents that were a mass of words and figures I didn't understand. It took another three meetings that autumn before I was good enough to do it without his help. In that time we became friends. My first real friend, I guess. And now he's dead.

After a month he gave me his computer. The thought of having that wonderful machine on my own desk took my breath away. "I can't afford it!" I gasped.

"It's a gift," he said. "In future I want you to work from home and do hacking for me. I'm ready to upgrade to a new computer anyway. You may as well have this old one."

"But why? What sort of work?" I asked.

"You've seen the way I hack into company computers?"

"Yes."

"I get information on things like sales figures. If a company does really well then people who have shares in it can make a fortune. The trick is to know a company is doing well *before* the rest of the public know. I simply sell that information to my contacts. It's harmless."

"It's spying. It's illegal," I said.

He looked at me, then his restless eyes flickered away. "It's just a game," he said. "You can make hundreds of Deutschmarks a month."

"Why don't you do it and make the money for yourself?" I asked. "Why give it to me?"

"Because I haven't time for this spying into companies. I have other things to do with my computer time."

"What things?"

He chewed on his lip for a while then said, "Let's see how you get on with this. I'll let you into my little secret another time. OK?"

I shrugged. I was too excited at the idea of making a fortune to think about Karl's schemes. I trusted him. He was my friend, but now he's dead.

My part of the deal worked perfectly. I hacked and stole and sneaked my way into computers around the world to find the information I needed. I loaded it on to floppy disks, passed it to Karl and an envelope stuffed with money arrived within a week. I'd never seen so much money. I didn't dare tell my parents what I was doing and I didn't have anything I wanted to spend the money on. I just pushed it into my dressing-table drawer under my clean socks.

It was like Karl said. A game. Unreal. Until one day I received a message from Karl. "Come and see me. Make sure you're not followed. If anyone is watching my flat then turn around and go home."

We'd been sending messages through the computers for months. It would be strange to see him face to face again.

It was winter now, of course, and snow was drifting down out of a colourless sky as I climbed on the bus. A few people got on the bus at the same stop. More got on and left at various stops along the road. No one got off at the stop nearest Karl's house. Whatever was going on, I was sure I wasn't being followed. A silver Audi car stopped at the end of the road and snapped off its headlights as I stepped off the bus. I guessed they could have followed by car if they had been watching my house.

I stayed at the stop as if I was waiting for another bus to come along. After a few minutes the Audi pulled away and drove past me. I was alone in the street outside Karl's flat. Anyone with any sense was indoors, out of the freezing wind. I crossed the road and looked over my shoulder before I pressed the buzzer on the entrance to Karl's block of flats. Anyone could have been watching from any of the darkened windows of the houses opposite. It was a chance I had to take.

The door buzzed and I stepped inside. The warmth of the central heating wrapped itself around me and I took the lift up to the third floor.

Karl was waiting by the door. His face was paler than ever and his expression bleak. Even his restless eyes seemed frozen in some helplessness. "What's wrong?" I asked.

"I've been tricked," he said over his shoulder as he led the way into his computer room. He sat on the swivel chair by the keyboard and rocked slowly backwards and forwards.

"What happened?" I asked.

"I was making a good living from spying on company secrets – the way you are now. But it was too easy," he said and his voice was dull. "I wasn't greedy. I just wanted a challenge. I wanted to hack into the world's greatest secrets just to prove I could do it. Like a mountain climber would want to climb Everest, just to prove themselves."

"What sort of secrets?"

"Military secrets," he said.

And he told me what he'd been doing for the last few months. "I found ways into most of the United States Military research bases. I've hacked into the latest weapon system secrets, into NASA's space programme, into the Central Intelligence Agency's spy network and into the FBI records. There is hardly a secret in the USA that I couldn't get at sooner or later."

"And Russia and China?" I asked.

He turned away from me. "No, not them."

Suddenly I understood. "You've been spying for the Russians? Passing your data to their spies?"

"The KGB," he nodded.

"And now you've been found out?"

"I ... I think so. I never stayed connected to a secret file too long. I didn't want the Americans to be able to trace me. Then I came across a new, huge batch of secrets in a file called SDINET. It would take me a long time to load that file on to my computer, but the KGB ordered me to do it."

"Even if it meant you getting caught?"

"They said they'd protect me."

"You think the Americans are on to you now? Then ask the KGB to help," I said. I couldn't see the problem.

"It seems this SDINET information was rubbish. It was just a collection of old, useless material. It was just cheese in a trap and I was the mouse. The KGB are furious – the CIA are on their way to get me, they reckon, and Russia doesn't want to get the blame. I'm on my own."

"That's awful!" I cried.

"I was well paid – while it lasted," he sighed. "Now I have to take my punishment. Quite a few years in jail. But that's not why I asked you to come around."

In the next hour he showed me how to destroy all the memory on the computer I had back at home. "The CIA will want to know my contacts. I've wiped out every trace of you on this computer. You need to do the same at your end. Understand?"

"Yes, Karl. Thanks."

He gave a weak smile. "There's no point in us both being dragged down. Now go, destroy that information, but make sure no one is following you."

I rose to leave. "Is there no way to save yourself?" I asked.

"I'm a computer spy – an armchair agent. I'm not one of the spies you read about in books – on the run with a poison capsule under my tongue and a gun in my pocket. I wouldn't know where to start. No, Peter. If you can save yourself I'll be happy. Good luck."

We shook hands one last time and I let myself out into the winter night.

For the next month my parents were amazed to find me leaving my computer every night to watch the television news. It was January before a serious newsreader announced, "German police have uncovered a computer spy ring in Hanover that is alleged to have stolen thousands of secret documents electronically and passed them on to KGB Agents in Berlin..."

The police were taking the credit but everyone knew the American Secret Service was behind the arrests. I followed the case in the newspapers and was relieved to see they released Karl at Easter before he came to trial in May. If he was free to return home they can't have thought he was such a dangerous criminal after all.

It all seemed so hopeful. My spirits raised and I even tried a little computer hacking, just for fun.

When the news came through that he had failed to report to the police, I cheered. He had made a run for it at last – his KGB friends must have finally helped him out, I decided.

Then, a week later, he was found, what was left of him. The reporter said police were treating it as suicide. His car was found abandoned in a lonely wood. Nearby they saw Karl's charred body. It had been soaked in petrol and set on fire.

There were murmurs about this being a strange form of suicide. Who would want to die horribly like that? But no one mentioned the word "murder".

I read every newspaper report, word for word, and even used my computer to sift through the details. Look at them for yourself. He died with no shoes on and no shoes in the car – who would drive 20 miles without shoes?

There were scorch marks round the body but nowhere else – had he lain perfectly still while he burned?

His contacts in the computer spy ring had given all they knew to the police and knew that in return they would go free – so why on earth would Karl want to kill himself?

I've thought about it and worried about it for ten years now. I know that he was murdered. Spying is a dangerous business and failures often die. I know my friend was murdered. There's just one thing I don't know. Which side killed him – the Americans or the Russians?

Somewhere, hidden deep in a computer file in Moscow or in Washington, there is the answer. The only way I'll ever find out is if I get into that file and read it. I'm as good at hacking now as Karl ever was. I'm ready to start searching for the truth from the comfort of my armchair in front of this keyboard. I'm ready to become a hacker and a spy. Karl would like that.

If I disappear, then end up a blackened corpse, you'll know I've failed. But I have to try.

After all, Karl was my friend, and now he's dead.

Spying today is not what it was when agents were dropped by parachutes into enemy territory or lived in enemy camps and slipped coded messages out. Today spies need different skills...

F
A
C
T

F
I
L
E

Modern Spies

1. **Computer hacking.** If enemies can connect their computers to your computer then they can read all the secrets you've stored. In 1975, the US Navy was worried about enemy agents "hacking" into its computer, so it decided to spy on itself! "Tiger" teams were set up, which had to try and hack into the Navy's most secret files. The tiger teams broke into, and took over, every single computer system they tried to enter.

2. **Computer viruses.** If you can't read an enemy's secret files then the next best thing you can do is destroy them so he can't read them either. Some computer programs can be fed into an enemy computer to wipe out the records, or change them so the computer gives out false commands that confuse the enemy.

3. **Computer bugs.** America's Federal Bureau of Investigation (FBI) used a bug to find a traitor in their country's Central Intelligence Agency. From 1985 the man, Aldrich Ames, had been giving the Russians the names of American spies, and at least ten of them died as a result. The FBI won't say how they uncovered his treachery, but it is

F A C T   F I L E

believed the keyboard of his computer was fitted with a special bug. Every key he tapped sent a signal to an FBI computer so they got instant copies of all his letters as soon as he wrote them. In 1994 he was arrested and went to prison for life.

4. **Spy satellites.** Spies no longer need to cross borders to get the pictures they need. In 1959 the USA began using cameras in satellites to take pictures over enemy territory. They were simple things at first – the camera took a roll of film, the film was ejected, parachuted down to the Pacific Ocean and snatched in mid-air by a US aeroplane. (It couldn't be reloaded but 1,000 metres of film showed 1.6 million square miles of Soviet territory!) Now cameras beam pictures directly back to earth and can spot items as small as one metre across; heat-image cameras can also see objects five metres below the sands of the Sahara Desert.

5. **Satellite bugs.** There is no need for a spy to break into an enemy's office and plant a bug. Spy satellites can now fly high over the target and pick up radio and telephone messages on the ground below.

Is this the end of the spy? Will he or she just become some computer expert sitting behind a desk and learning everything they need to know from spy machines?

Look at what happened in the Gulf War in 1991. Iraq, led by Saddam Hussein, invaded the country next door – Kuwait.

Britain and America went to the aid of Kuwait and drove the invaders back. They used all the spy equipment available to help their armies, navies and air forces drive the Iraqis back. Spy satellites told the British and US armies exactly where Iraqi troops were moving and guided missiles and bombs on to targets.

But remember, the spy satellites didn't warn the US and British that the Iraqis were planning an invasion. It would have needed a man or woman close to Saddam Hussein's headquarters to warn of that. It would have needed a human spy. Their days are not over yet.

EPILOGUE

Spying isn't what it used to be. Spies aren't what they used to be.

In the past no one except the spies' masters knew who they were or where they worked. You couldn't just walk up to spy headquarters and apply for a job. You would not expect to see an advert in a newspaper saying, "Spies wanted."

But now you can!

In May 1997, the British Military Intelligence Agency put an advert in national newspapers and it invited people to apply for a job with them. Spies have been caught and suffered horrible deaths – tortured, shot, hanged and poisoned. Who on earth would want a job like that? Well, in the first week after the advert appeared more than 20,000 people applied.

If the 20,000 who applied think they are going to end up like James Bond, then they will be disappointed. The "super-powers" of the United States and Russia are at peace. In the 1960s they raced to be the first nation to have rockets in space. Now the American astronauts and Russian cosmonauts share a space station and work side by side. No more space-race secrets and no need for spies to steal those secrets.

America is also very open about its spy operations these days. Central Intelligence Agency files are open to anyone in the world on the Internet. Every week 120,000 people connect to the CIA site on:

http://www.odci.gov/cia/index.html

and more connect to the FBI on:

http://www.fbi.gov

Of course the CIA has its own "Internet" for the really secret material that the public can't read.

But there are still enemies at work and there are still secrets that need to be protected or uncovered. There are terrorists who want to assassinate leaders and destroy cities. There are drug dealers who want to smuggle dangerous substances and destroy lives. There are international criminals who smuggle everything from money and jewels to computer software and people. The police work hard to stop them, but it is so much easier if they know what these enemies of the state are planning next. We still need spies.

And spying is still terribly dangerous. Suppose a spy pretends to be a terrorist and finds out where they are hiding weapons – he or she will somehow have to pass on that information to the law officers. If he or she is caught passing on that information then the terrorists are not likely to be merciful.

Some things never change. As long as there are evil people planning harm to us then we need spies to help us stop them. Spies have always been seen as ruthless people who can't be trusted. But the truth is, spies can be the best friends we could ever wish for.

DON'T MISS THESE
GRIPPING CRIME STORIES

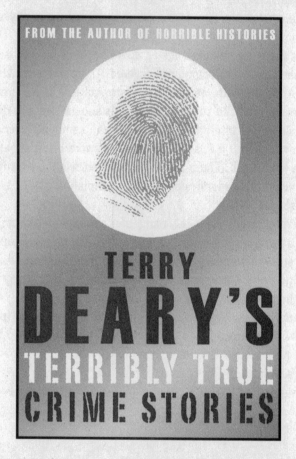
**They're guaranteed to bring out
the super sleuth in you!**